Vabella Publishing
P.O. Box 1052
Carrollton, Georgia 30112
www.vabella.com

©Copyright 2022 Robert Kenimer

All rights reserved. No part of the book may be reproduced or utilized in any form or by any means without permission in writing from the author. All requests should be addressed to the publisher.

Manufactured in the United States of America

ISBN 978-1-957479-33-0

For my daughters, Julie, Marla and Ellen who taught me the importance of children's books.

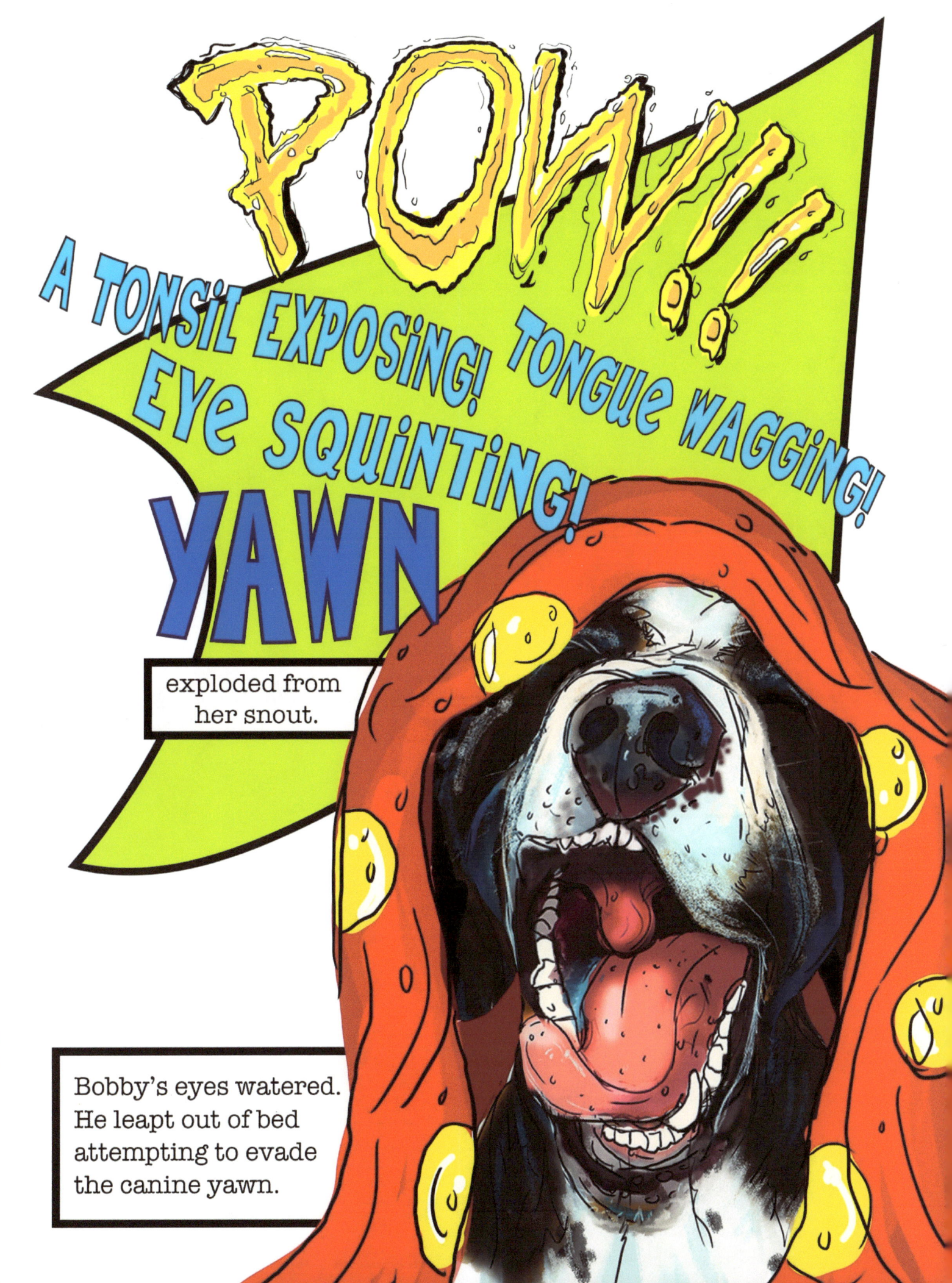

Winky's teacher, Miss Mallory, helped her with a carton of milk at lunch. Winky opened her mouth to shout thank you over the noisy lunchroom crowd, but instead . . .

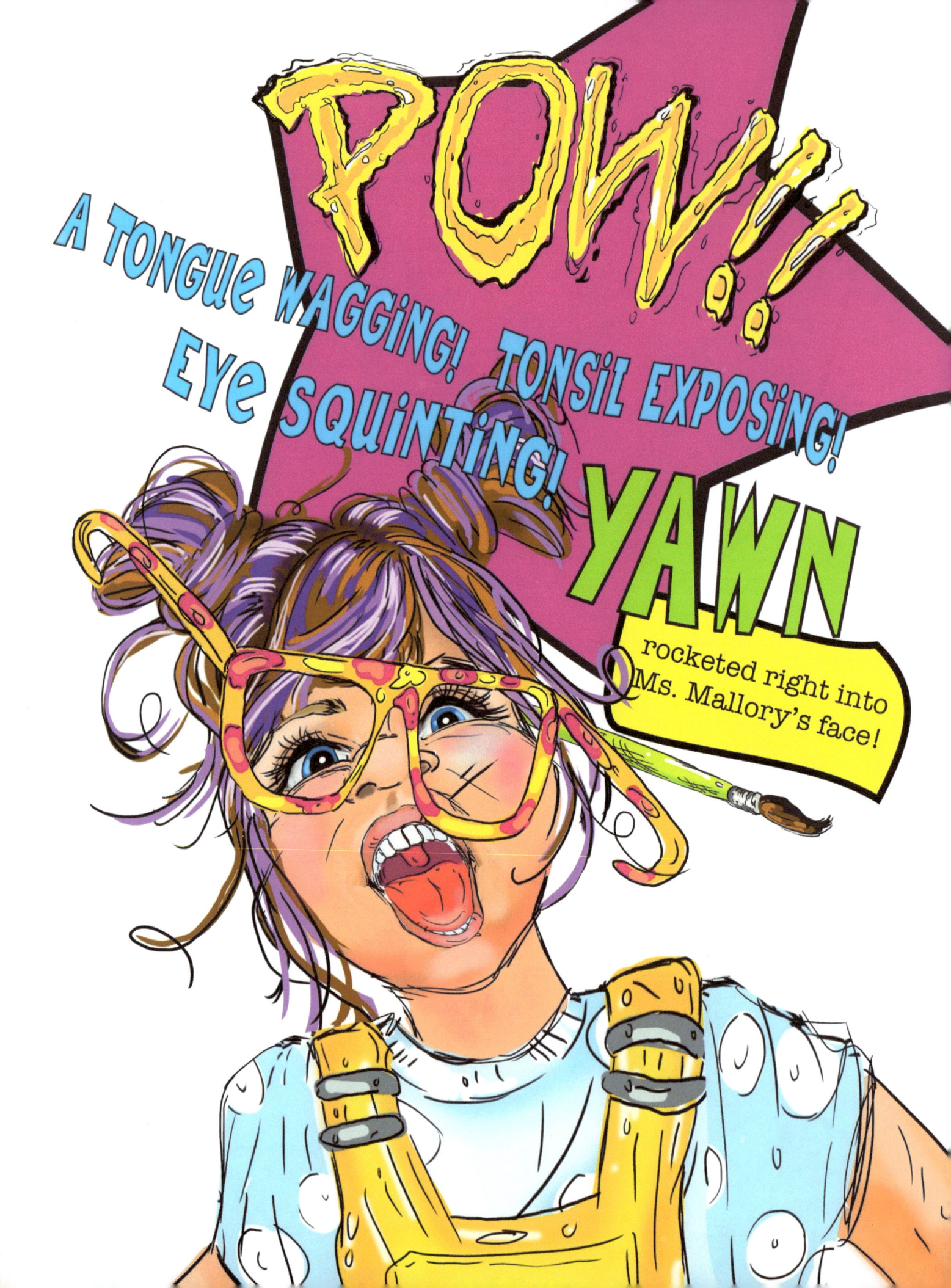

Miss Julie almost dropped Miss Mallory's bag of snacks. She gritted her teeth and mustered a silly grin, working to strangle the yawn from forcing her lips open.

The dancing, school crossing guard stopped Miss Julie on her way home from work. Miss Ellen waved for her to continue crossing.

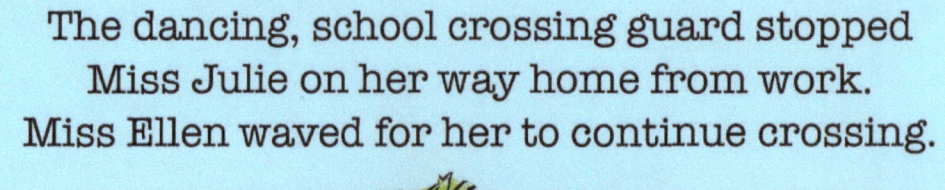

When she reached the school crossing guard, Miss Julie lost her battle with the yawns . . .

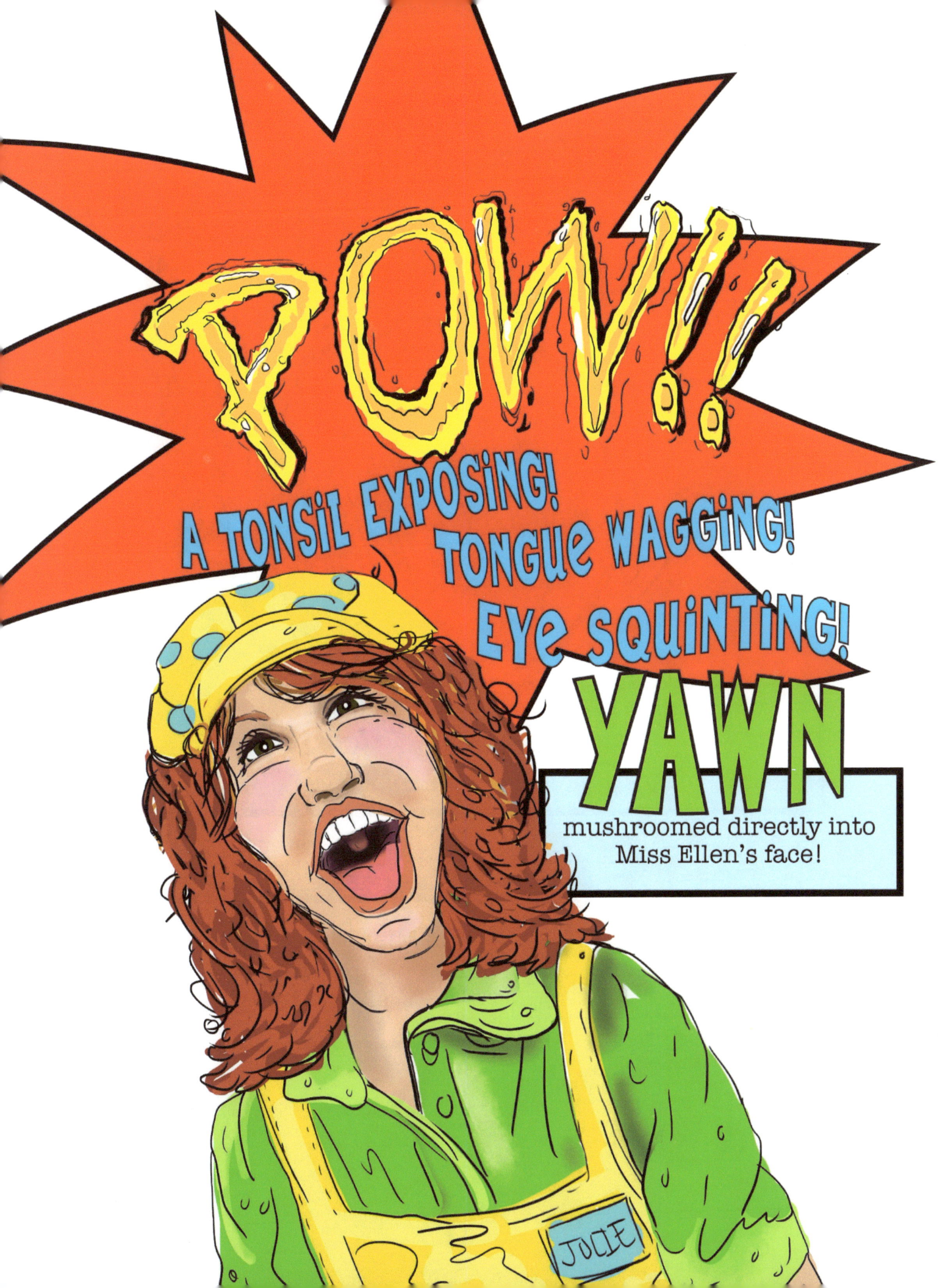

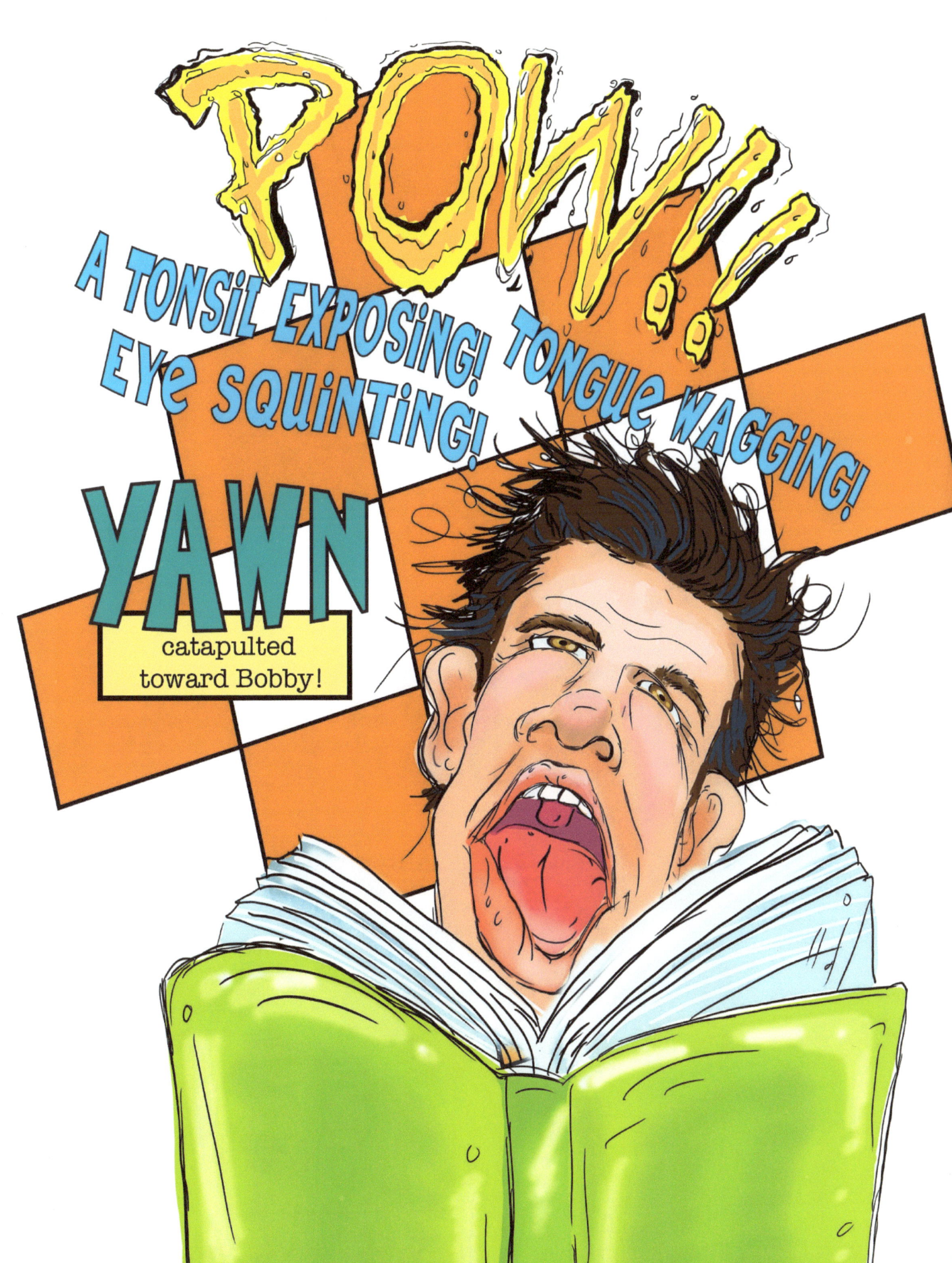

"I wonder where yawns come from?" he whispered as he fell asleep dreaming of yawning.

- How many times did you yawn while reading the book?

- How many yawns do you remember in the book? Go back and count them.

- Is it polite to yawn into someone else's face?

- Why do you yawn after seeing someone else yawn?

- What do you think Bobby dreamed about that night?

Author Robert Kenimer

One of the questions that has puzzled me over the decades is where do yawns come from. At this point, science has not determined the reason we yawn.

Personally...I think they are an alien life form that survives by jumping from person to person!

I hope you enjoyed THE BIG YAWN!

Illustrator Stacy Jordon

Stacy lives in Georgia with her husband Billy. She has been a Professional Artist for over thirty years.
www.artbystacyj.com

Find your "Happy Place" and set up Camp!

A Happy Heart makes the face cheerful...
Proverbs 15:13 NIV

CPSIA information can be obtained
at www.ICGtesting.com
Printed in the USA
BVHW020611260922
647568BV00002BA/10